W9-DFP-092

Other Little Rooster Books you will enjoy:

MY MOM MADE ME GO TO CAMP, Judy Delton
THE SCHOOL TRIP, Nick Butterworth and Mick Inkpen
FIELD DAY, Nick Butterworth and Mick Inkpen

MY MOM MADE ME GO TO SCHOOL
A Little Rooster Book / published by arrangement with Delacorte Press
PUBLISHING HISTORY
Delacorte edition published 1991

Bantam edition / July 1993

Little Rooster is a trademark of Bantam Books, a division of
Bantam Doubleday Dell Publishing Group, Inc.

ISBN 0-553-37252-1

Printed simultaneously in the United States and Canada

Bantam Books are published by Bantam Books, a division of Bantam Doubleday
Dell Publishing Group, Inc. Its trademark, consisting of the words "Bantam
Books" and the portrayal of a rooster, is Registered in U.S. Patent and
Trademark Office and in other countries. Marca Registrada. Bantam Books,
1540 Broadway, New York, New York 10036.

PRINTED IN THE UNITED STATES OF AMERICA

UPR   0 9 8 7 6 5 4 3 2 1

For Daniel,
My favorite
grandchild,
J.D.

To my dad
with love,
L.M.

My Mom Made Me
Go to School

by Judy Delton
pictures by Lisa McCue

A BANTAM LITTLE ROOSTER BOOK

NEW YORK · TORONTO · LONDON · SYDNEY · AUCKLAND

The day after my birthday my mom said,
"Summer is over. This year you start
school. You'll learn how to read and write.
How to add and how to spell."

"I don't want to spell," I said.

"You will ride the school bus," said my
mom. "And meet new friends."

"Lars is my friend," I said. "One friend is
enough."

The next morning my mom made me go
shopping.
"You need brand-new clothes for school,"
she said.

"I've got clothes," I said. "I've got jeans. The
ones with the holes in the knees."
My mom made me try on corduroy pants.
They smelled awful. They were green like
peas and they didn't bend. They were too
big and they hung over my shoes. They
were pants for a giant.

"We'll take them," said my mom. "You'll
grow a lot this year. These will last a long
time."

I groaned.

My mom bought me a shirt that had
stripes. They went across, the wrong way.

Then we went to the shoe department.
The salesperson measured my feet. He
made me put on shoes that pinched my
toes. They didn't bend either.

"A perfect fit!" said the salesperson.

When we got home, I decided to run away. I packed my race cars and a peanut-butter sandwich. I took my World Series jacket in case I ended up in Alaska, where it was cold. I took my ball and my bat.

"Good-bye!" I said to my room. "Good-bye!" I said to my wrong-way shirt and my shoes that pinched.

I went out the back door forever.

Then I wondered where to go. The library was closed. I called for Lars but he wasn't home. My grandma lived in Minneapolis. I couldn't go there without a bus ticket.

"I suppose I can live in the doghouse," I said. It was a big doghouse. There was enough room for my dog, Clyde, and me.

"Arf!" said Clyde. He didn't like to be squished.

"Archie!" called my mom. (That's my name, Archie.) "Come and eat!"

I didn't want to eat. I didn't want to go in the house. And I didn't want to go to school. No one could make me. But I went inside anyway.

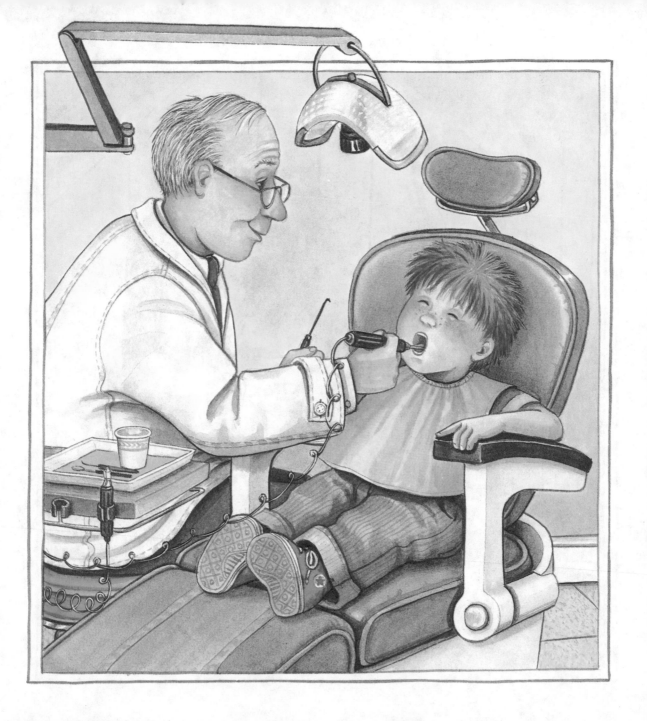

The next day my mom made me go to the
dentist.
"It's a before-school checkup," she said.

"It's a no-school checkup," I told the
dentist.

"Open wide," said the dentist.
He put some pink stuff in my mouth. He
told my mom I'd better floss. Then he
polished my teeth with a machine.
"You'll have the shiniest snappers in
kindergarten!" he said.

(That's what he thinks.)

After that we went to the doctor. She gave me booster shots and a lollipop.

"We're all set for kindergarten!" she said. She may be all set. But I'm not. I'm not going to school. My mom can't make me.

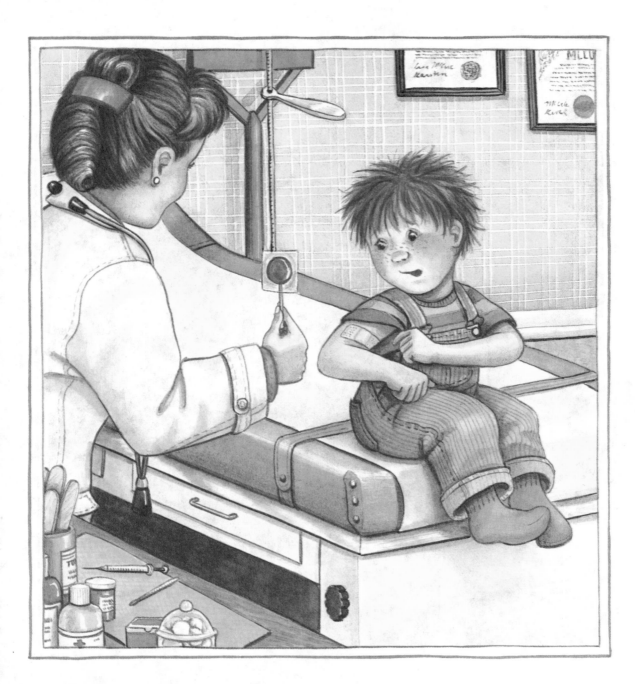

The next morning my mom made me get my hair cut.

"No!" I screamed. I put my hands over my head. I hid under the bed. "I like my hair!" I shouted. "I don't want to be bald."

"All the kids get their hair cut before school," said my mom.

"Not me," I said. "Because I'm not going to school."

The barber's name was Max. He used a
machine on my head that hummed and
tickled. When he finished, my head felt
like a toothbrush. My ears looked too big.

"Good luck at school!" called the barber
when we left.
I don't need luck, I thought. Because I
won't be at school. I'll be in my own
backyard playing with my toy race cars.

On Monday my mom got pencils and crayons and a tablet. (I can always color at home.)
On Tuesday she got Twinkies for a school snack. (I can always eat them at home in the kitchen.)

On Wednesday my mom said, "Hurry up,
Archie, or you'll be late for school!"
(I hid in the closet.)

"I'll drive you today," she said. "Tomorrow
you and Lars can take the school bus."

Tomorrow I'll find a better place to hide, I
thought. A place where my mom can't find me.

My new pants whistled when I walked. My shoes were making blisters on my feet. All the kids would laugh. (At my short hair and big ears.)

"I'm not going to school!" I said to Lars. His mom was in the front seat with my mom.

"Then you're in the wrong car," he said back.

We went into a room with a K on the door. The teacher said, "Welcome to kindergarten!" There was a chair with my name on it. It said "Archie" on a blue card that was shaped like a race car.

My mom went home. Lars's mom left too.

I raised my hand. "Do we have to spell?" I said.

The teacher laughed. "Not this year."

After rest-time a kid came up to me.
"My name is Martin," he said.

"Mine is Archie," I said back. "Do you like
race cars?"

"Yeah, come on over to my house this
afternoon and see my cars."

"Can Lars come too?"

"Yeah," said Martin.

After school my mom was waiting. "How was school?" she asked.

"We don't have to spell," I said. "My teacher's name is Ms. Hill. Can I go over to Martin's to see his race cars?"

"After you change your clothes," she said.

I put on my old jeans. The ones with the holes in the knees. And my old sneakers that never pinched my toes. Then I started for Martin's house. Lars came too.

"One day of school is okay," I told him. "But I'm not going back tomorrow. Nobody can make me."

Judy Delton has written more than sixty-five books for young readers, including *My Mom Made Me Go to Camp* and the Dell Young Yearling books about the Pee Wee Scouts. She lives in St. Paul, Minnesota.

Lisa McCue has illustrated several books for children, including *My Mom Made Me Go to Camp* by Judy Delton. She lives in Bethlehem, Pennsylvania.